SCOOP
Copyright © 2007, CTC Publishing, LLC

Author: Julia Cook
Illustrator: Elisabeth Ventling
Designed by: Chris O'Connor

Printed in the U.S.A.

Summary: This book teaches children personal safety.

ISBN10: 1-934073-07-5
ISBN13: 978-1-934073-07-0

Published by: CTC Publishing
10431 Lawyers Rd.
Vienna, VA 22181
Voice: (703) 319-0107
Fax: (703) 319-0551
Website: www.ctcpub.com

This book is dedicated to Spencer,
a true hero who NEVER gives up!

I was outside playing with Zippy, my new baby rabbit, when I heard my Mama calling me.

3

I carefully set Zippy down into a cardboard box and ran inside the house to see what she wanted.

4

Mama made me sit down in the "Talk To" chair. Mama always has a lot to say, but when you have to sit down in the "Talk To" chair, you know what she's about to say is *very* important.

Mama said it was time for me to learn all about the "SCOOPER SAFETY RULES."

"People come in all shapes and sizes," said Mama.
"Some are large.
Some are scrawny.
Some are tall.
Some are short."

"Some people dress up in nice clothes.
Others wear ratty clothes.
Some have big hair.
Some have no hair.
Some people look strange,
and others look just fine."

"Our world is full of 'SAFE PEOPLE' that you can go to if you ever need help," said Mama.

"What does a SAFE PERSON look like?" I asked.

"A SAFE PERSON can be a Mama with children, a police officer, a fire fighter, a teacher, or a clerk working at a store," she said.

"Most people are nice and kind," said Mama. "But there are some people out there who are *scoopers*! A *scooper* is a person who scoops you up, takes you away from your family, and tries to hurt you! **A *scooper* can be a person that you know, or a person that you have never met before,**" she said.

"How can I tell?" I asked Mama. "How do I know if a person is a *scooper*?"

"You can't tell by looking at their outside," said Mama. "So you must always be very careful. You have to be smart and confident and learn to trust your instincts!"

"Trust my what?" I asked…

"Your instincts," said Mama. "You know, the 'Uh Oh' voice inside your head that tells you when things just aren't right."

Yesterday my neighbor, Mrs. Bridgman, came to pick me up
after school. My Mama hadn't told me that this was going
to happen. I would not leave with Mrs. Bridgman!
I turned around and went back inside the
office and used my call list.

"You should never go with anybody unless you check them out with someone on your call list," said Mama.

A call list is a list of people that I can call to make sure that I am making the right choice. My call list has three people and their phone numbers on it: my Mama, my Grandma, and my Uncle James. If a person ever asks or tells me to go with her, I ignore what she tells me, go to the nearest phone, and use my call list. If I can't get anyone on my call list to answer, I'm supposed to stay right by the phone and try my list again.

First, I called my Mama…no answer. Then I tried my Grandma. She answered and said that it was just fine for me to ride home with Mrs. Bridgman, so I did.

That night, I told my Mama what happened after school. "I am so proud of you for using your call list," said Mama. "Checking first is always the right thing to do."

"I think you're just a big Fraidy Cat," said my big brother, Myron. "Besides, you're too much of a brat to get scooped up by a *scooper*."

"You can never be too careful," said Mama. "Even brats can get scooped!"

"If a grown-up that you don't know very well tries to talk to you, and you are alone, you should not talk back to him. You should ignore him and walk away," said Mama. "Grown-ups shouldn't talk to kids that they don't know."

"A *scooper* may pretend to need your help," said Mama. "He might knock on our front door and say something like, " 'Hey, my car just broke down and my cell phone isn't working. Can you let me into your house so that I can use the phone?' "

"I would NEVER let anyone into our house, unless you were there to say its O.K.," I said. "I would ignore his knock and not talk to him at all."

"That's right!" said Mama. "If the person really needs help, he can try another house where a grown-up is at home."

"How can I tell if I know a grown-up well enough to talk to him?" I asked.

"You can always talk to 'SAFE PEOPLE'," said Mama. "But if you aren't sure, use the *'dinner guide.'* Would I invite the person who is talking to you over for dinner? If not, ignore what he is saying and walk away."

"A *scooper* needs your attention and might try to trick you into getting too close to her," said Mama. "She might say something like 'Hey, see my new puppy. Isn't he cute?' Then, when you kneel down to pet the puppy, she might scoop you up and take you away from our family!"

"No one can ever scoop you if they can't reach you," said Mama. "Always remember to listen to your 'Uh Oh' voice, ignore what the person says, and keep her **OUT** of your personal space."

"Personal space is so important!" said Mama. "Always keep a safe distance! No one can scoop you if they can't reach you!"

My Mama never lets me play in the park by myself. I always have to pair up with someone. Usually, I go with Myron. He's as strong as an OX!

19

A *scooper* would have a tough time scooping up Myron. When Mama tries to pick him up, she says he's nailed to the floor. Besides, Myron is very smart. He has a great "Uh Oh" voice, and he knows the **SCOOPER Safety Rules!**

"I wish all of the *scoopers* out there would wear name tags, so that I could tell who they were," I said.

"That would only happen in a perfect world," said Mama. "But if you stick to my five important **SCOOPER Safety Rules**, you'll be safe from scooping."

RULES

RULE 1. Be **Smart** and confident and trust your instincts. Always listen to your "Uh oh" voice.

RULE 2. Never go with anyone without checking it out on your **Call List** first.

RULE 3 **Zero Talking**. Don't talk to grown-ups that you don't know, especially when you are alone.

RULE 4. Keep people **out** of your personal space. Always keep a safe distance.

RULE 5. Never go places without a friend. **Pair Up** so that you are not alone.

"That is way too much for me to remember!" I said.
"Well," said my Mama, "I can help you with that."

She took my hand and with a marker wrote the letters
S C O O P on the tips of my fingers.

"What's that for?" I asked.

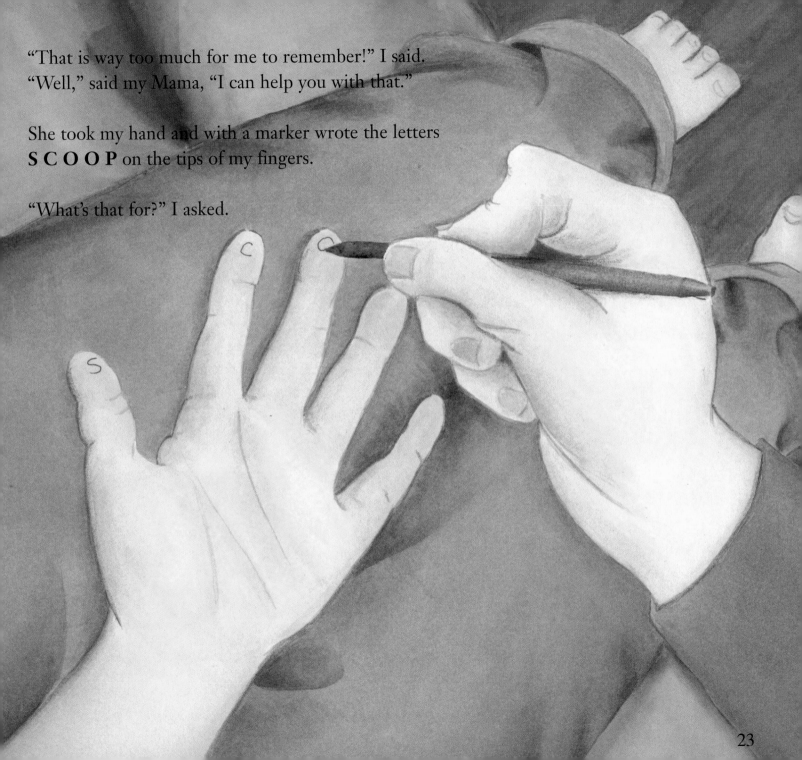

"The **S** stands for **SMART**:   Be smart and confident, and trust your instincts. Listen to your 'Uh Oh' voice."

"The **C** stands for **CALL LIST**:   Always call first so that you make the right choice."

"The **O** stands for zer**O** Talking: Do not talk to grown-ups that you don't know well, especially when you are alone."

"The other **O** stands for *OUT*:   Keep people *out* of your personal space."

"The **P** stands for **PAIR UP**:   Always go places with a friend."

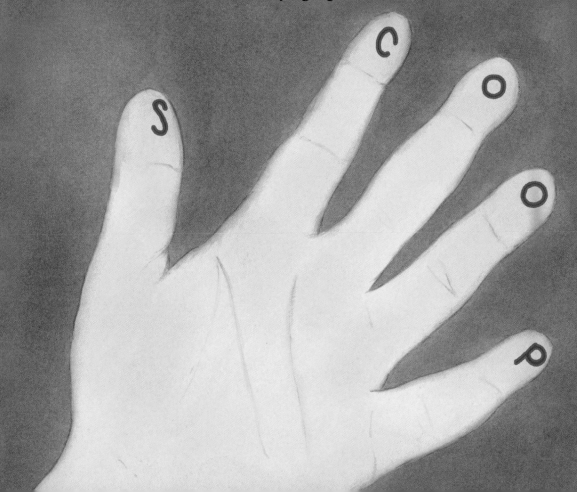

Mama smiled at me
and gave me a big hug.

"I love you so much!"
she said.

25

Then I went back outside and looked at the **SCOOP** on my fingertips, and I thought about all that Mama had said.

I looked into the cardboard box. There he was — my baby rabbit, my Zippy. He was perfect!
I had planned on keeping him as a pet. I had tricked him by putting carrots in my backyard,
and when he was busy eating, I scooped him up and took him away from his family.
My tummy started to get knots in it. To him, I had become a *scooper*!

I carried the box to my backyard and set it down softly in the grass. I lifted my baby rabbit out of the box and held him up to my face. "I'm really sorry for scooping you up and taking you away from your family," I said.

28

I set Zippy down carefully and waved goodbye to him. I watched closely as he quickly hopped back into the bushes...

...right back to his family where he belongs.

A Note to Parents and Educators:

There are some topics that we wish we never had to discuss with our children, abduction being one of them. Of course, we can choose to ignore the issue and simply hope it never happens. Another approach is to never let our children out of our sight. No one can advocate either of these strategies.

Most parents are eager to learn a simple and effective way to help protect their children from *"Scoopers."* When I was a child my parents told me not to take candy from strangers or get in a car with someone I didn't know. They had limited knowledge of this issue as did many other people. I can't ever remember hearing about a missing child as I was growing up. Today, the media have brought the issue to the public, for better, and for worse.

Parents constantly ask me, what do I need to do? Today, we need to empower our children with skills that will build their self-confidence in dealing with dangerous situations. We have to be careful not to tell our children that the world is full of scary people. Unfortunately, the news media do that for us. Rather, children need to know that most adults they encounter in their lives are basically good people. Parents and educators need to make child safety part of their everyday life by practicing and reviewing basic safety skills.

This book is an excellent way to start the dialogue and to open up our children's minds to the issue of luring prevention. Author Julia Cook has presented this subject in a manner that children will relate to. This book should be used as a tool to teach, renew, and practice the skills children need to know to keep them safe.

The child is usually the last line of defense against the "Scooper"!

Thanks, Julia for working with us to help keep our children safe!

Don Wood, Founder
Child Watch of North America

31

SAFETY RULES

For Children:

- Know your name, address, and phone number.
- Learn *how* and *when* to call 911.
- If you are scared of someone, RUN to safety.
- It's OK to be RUDE to a grown-up if you feel you are unsafe.
- Have a "Call List" and know how to use it.
- Don't let anyone on the phone or at the door know that you are home alone.
- If you ever get lost in a mall, stay where you are until you are found.
- Beware of an adult that asks you to keep a secret from your parents.
- Avoid shortcuts when you are walking from one place to another.
- If you are ever "scooped," scream, kick, bite, and fight as hard as you can to get away! Never *ever* trust what the "scooper" tells you.
- Tell your parents or a trusted adult if someone is asking you to do something that makes you feel uncomfortable. Listen to your "Uh Oh" voice.
- Review and practice these rules often.

For Parents:

- Don't ever leave children unattended in a vehicle, whether it is running or not.
- Make sure you know how to find or contact your children at all times.
- Take an active role in your children's activities.
- As tired as you may be, take the time to listen intently to your children when they tell you they had a bad dream. There could be a reason. Trust your instincts.
- Talk to your children about inappropriate incidences you hear on the news and get their perspective.
- Question and monitor anyone who takes an unusual interest in your children.
- Teach your children that they can be rude to an adult if they feel threatened in any way. They need to hear it from you directly because this message often contradicts everything they have heard before.
- Have your children practice their most annoying scream. They may need to use it someday.
- Check websites for registered offenders in your neighborhood. Talk to your children about why these people should be avoided.
- Practice and reinforce the safety rules at all times. Role-play and rehearse "what if" scenarios.

\